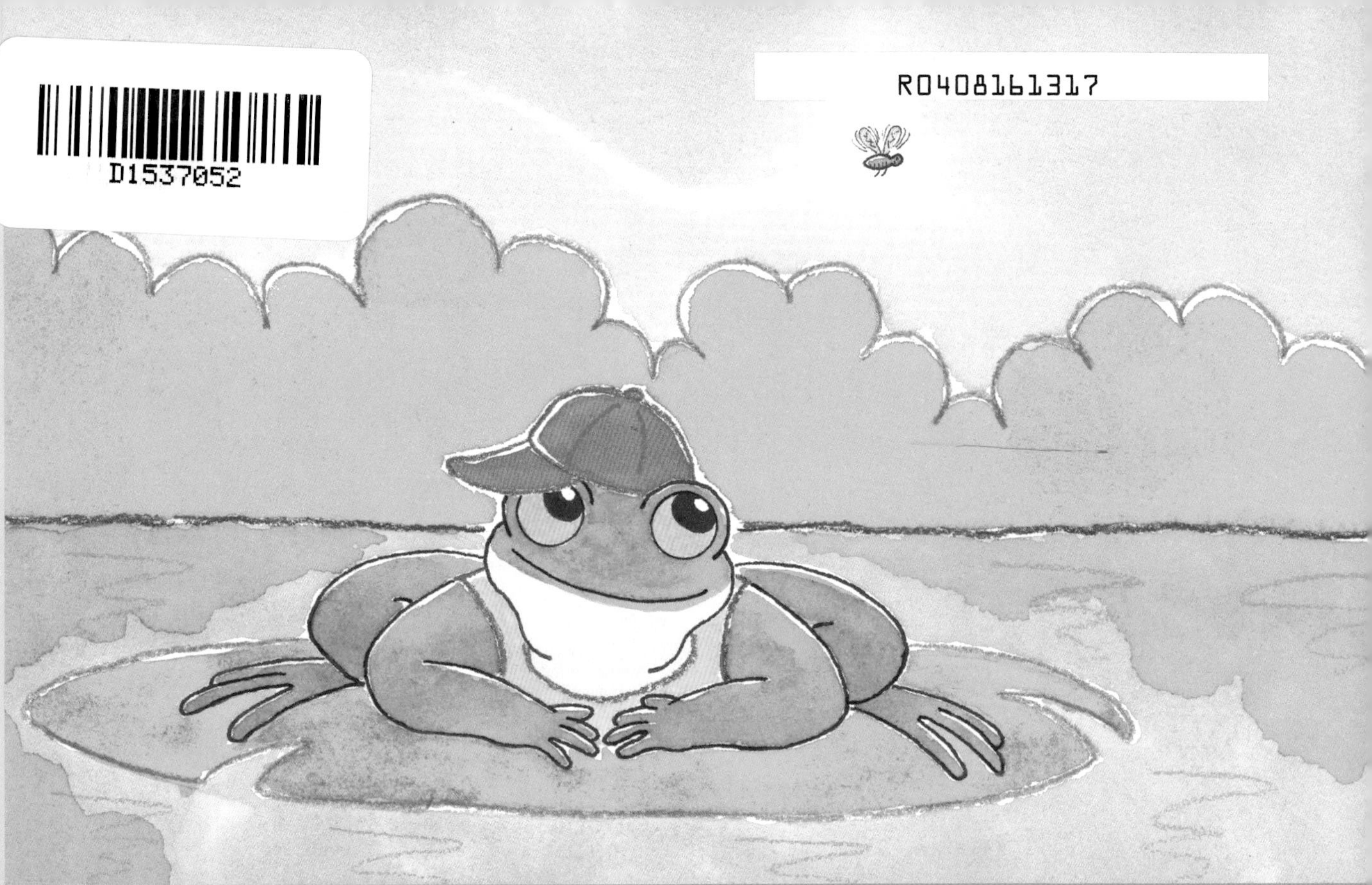

Bob sees a fly.

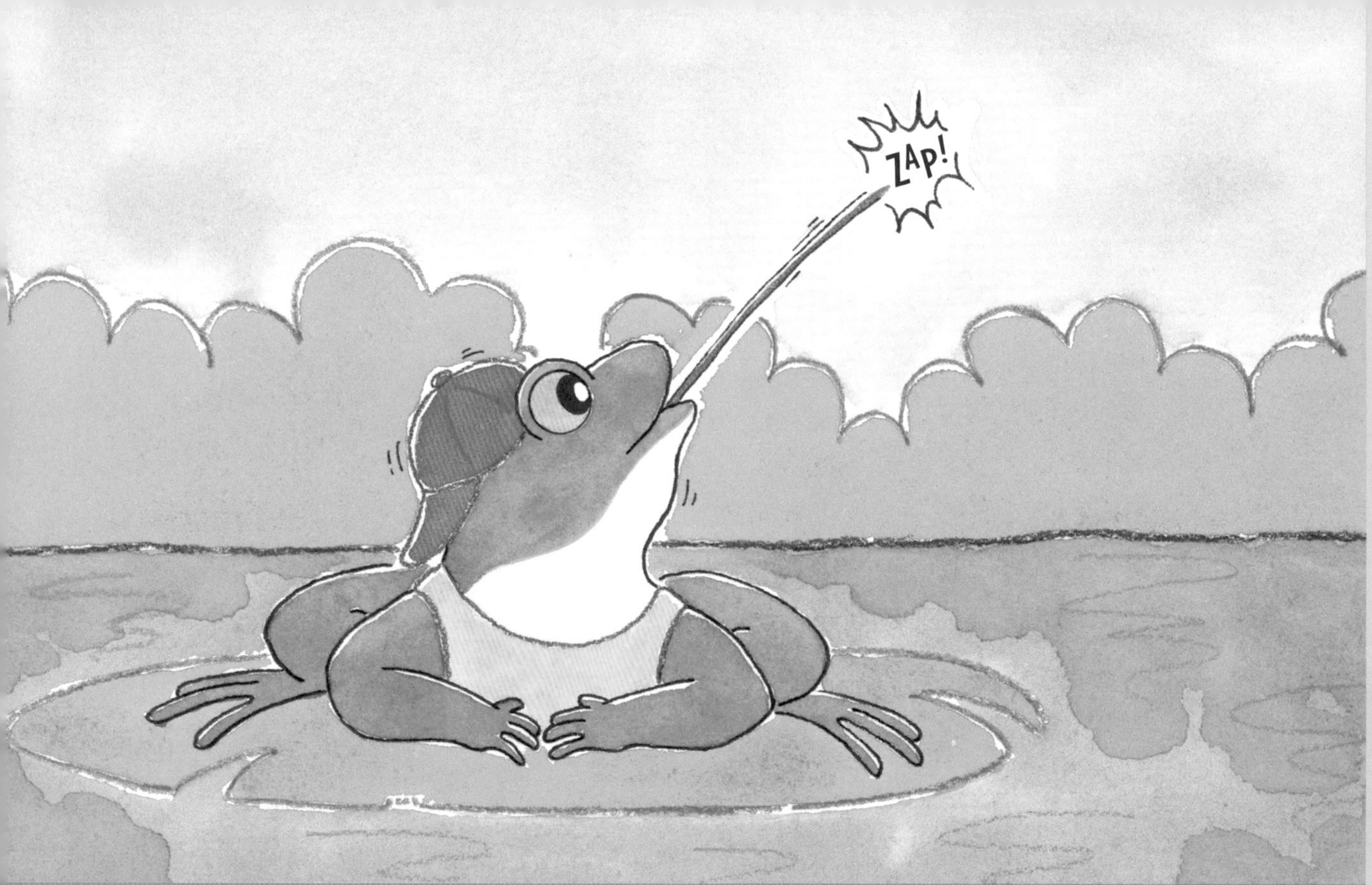

Zap! He catches it.

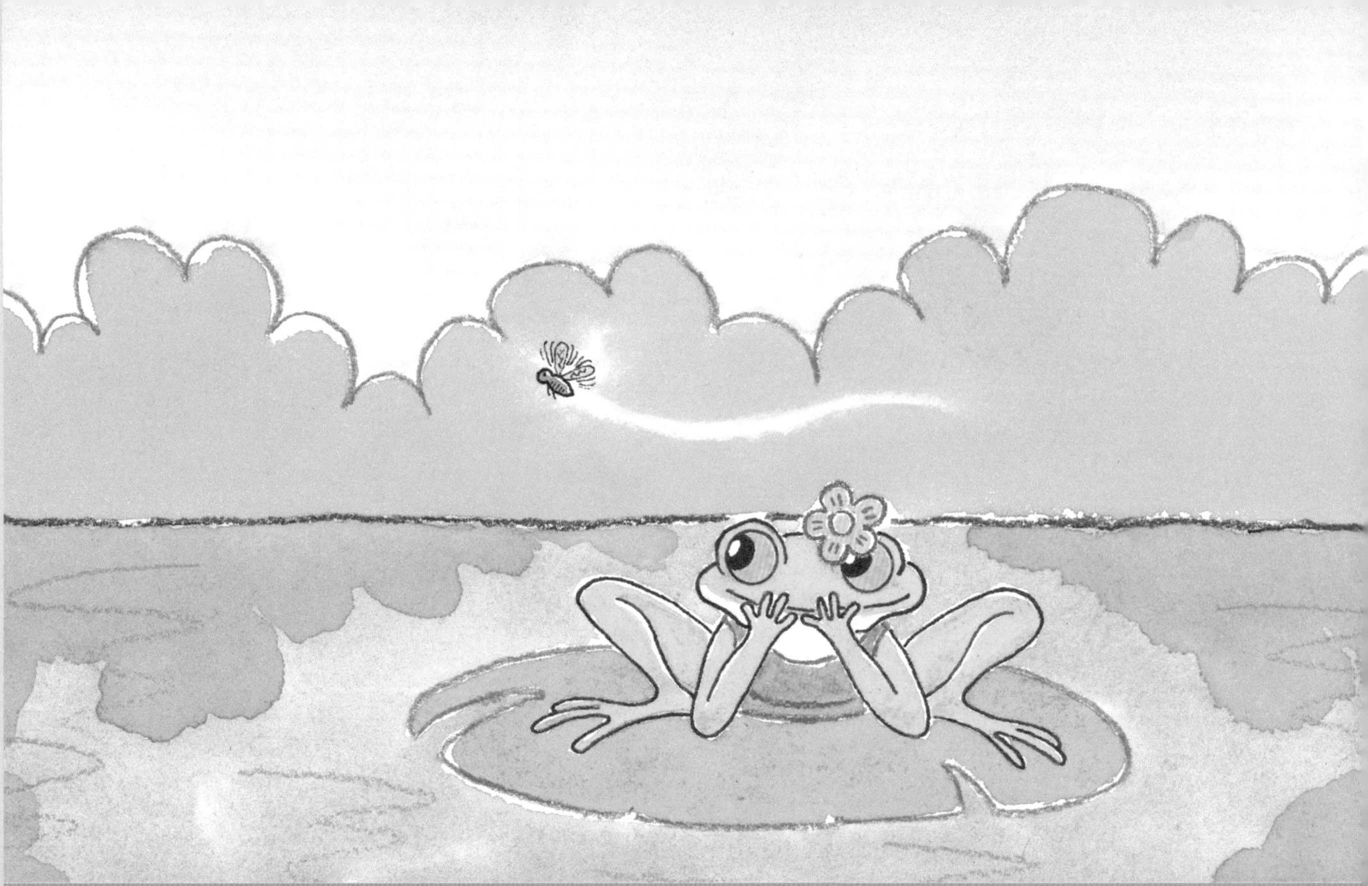

Lucy sees a fly.

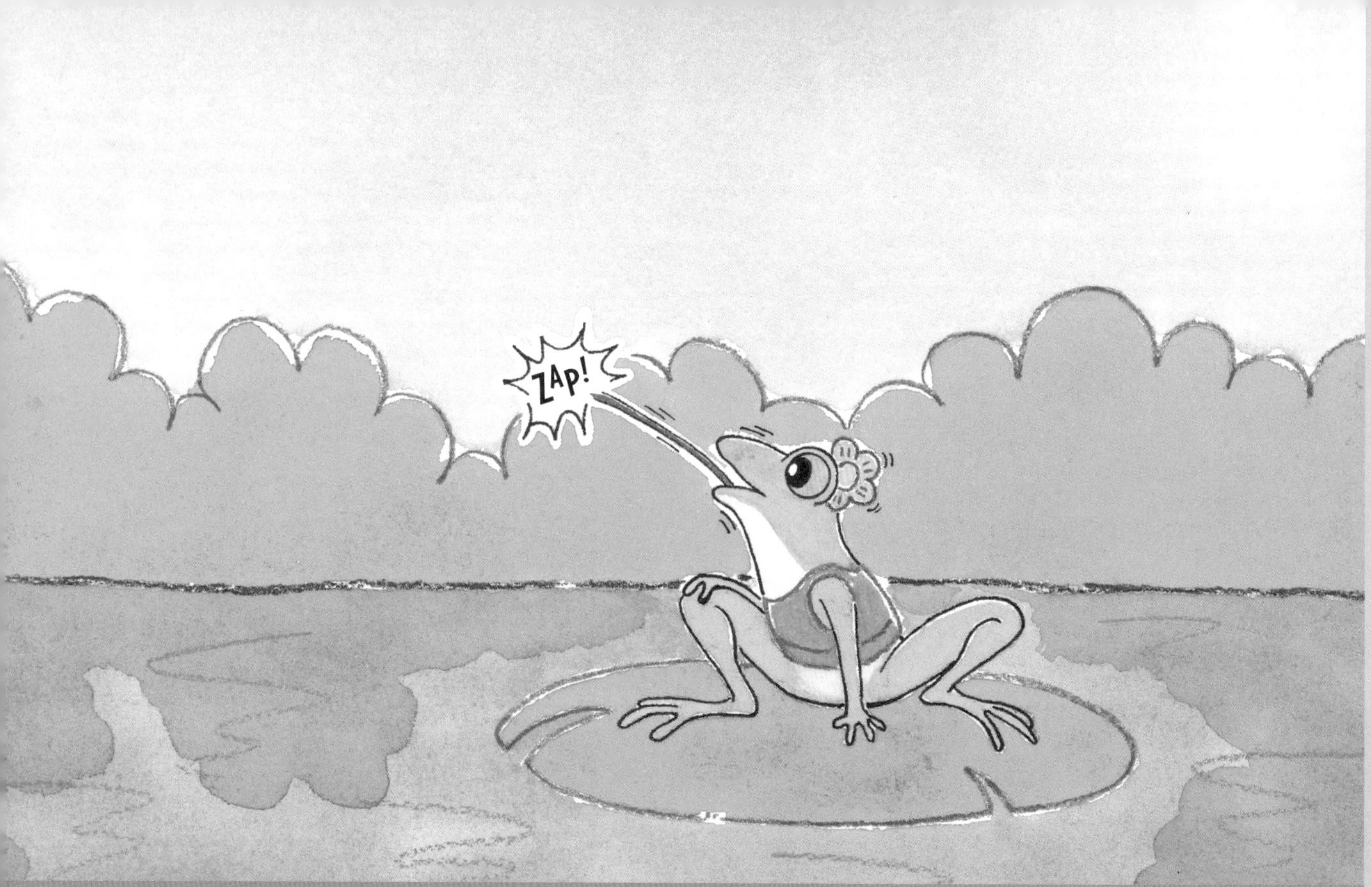

Zap! She catches it.

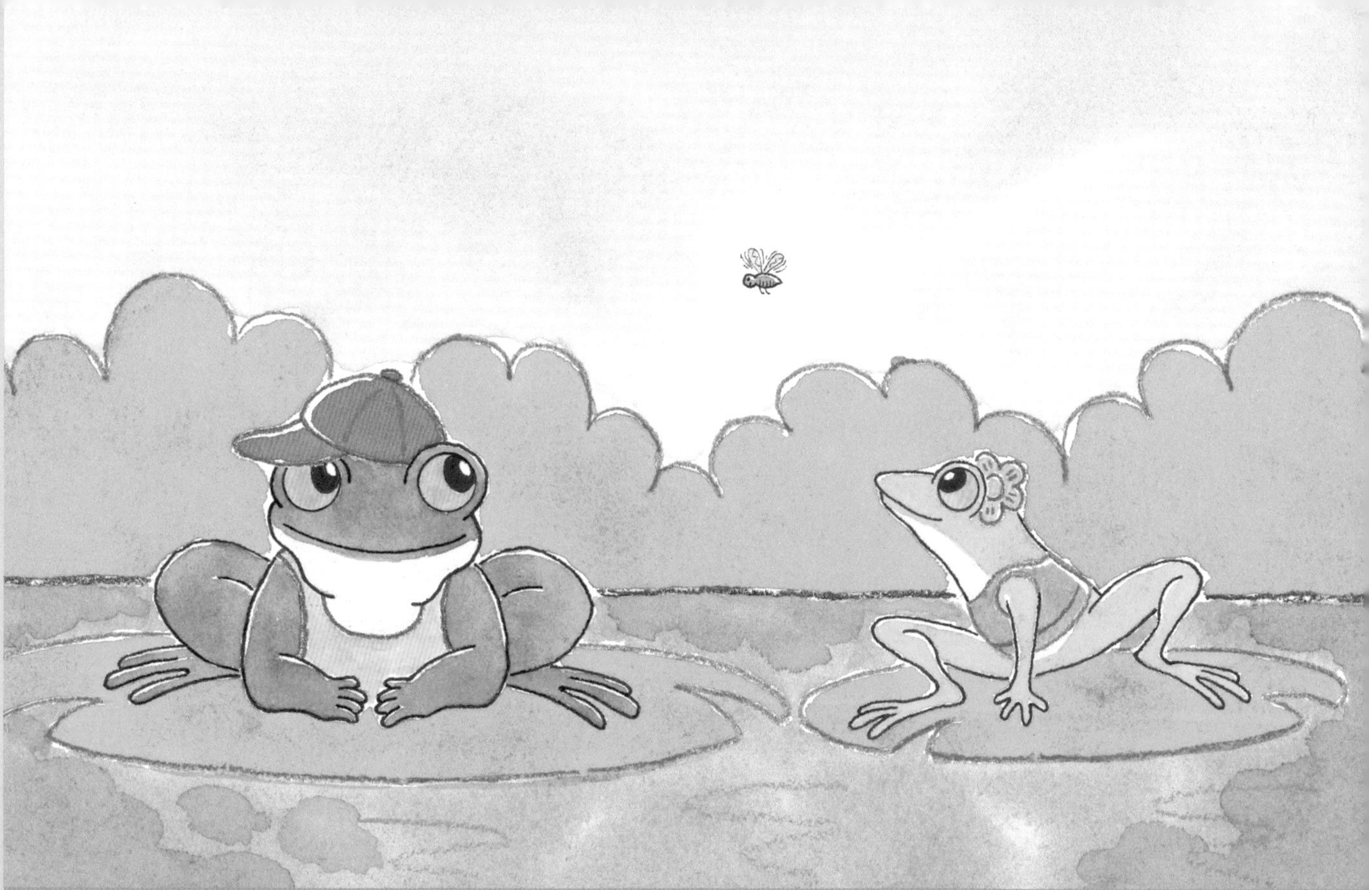

Bob and Lucy see another fly.

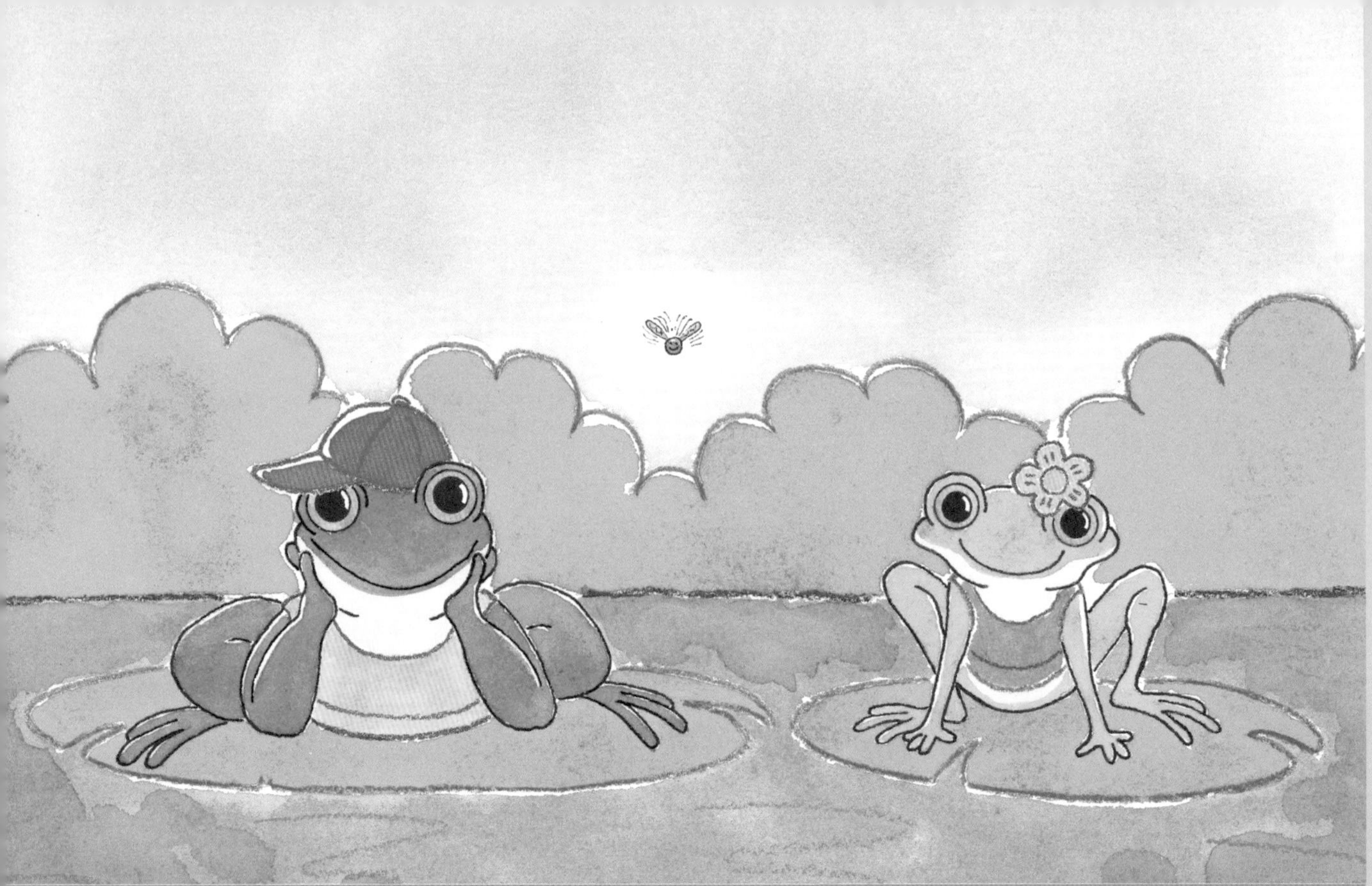

Bob and Lucy smile.

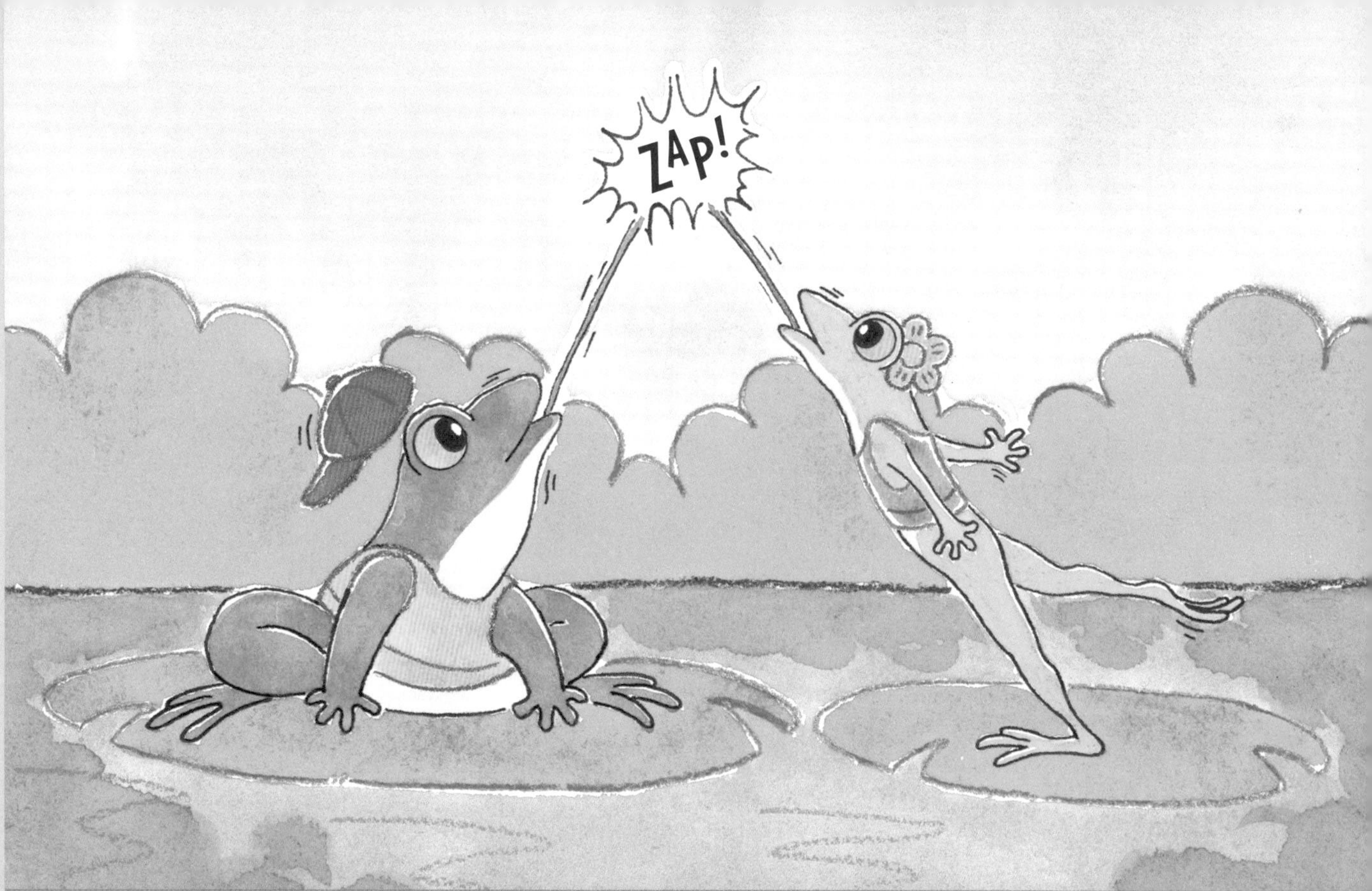

Zap!

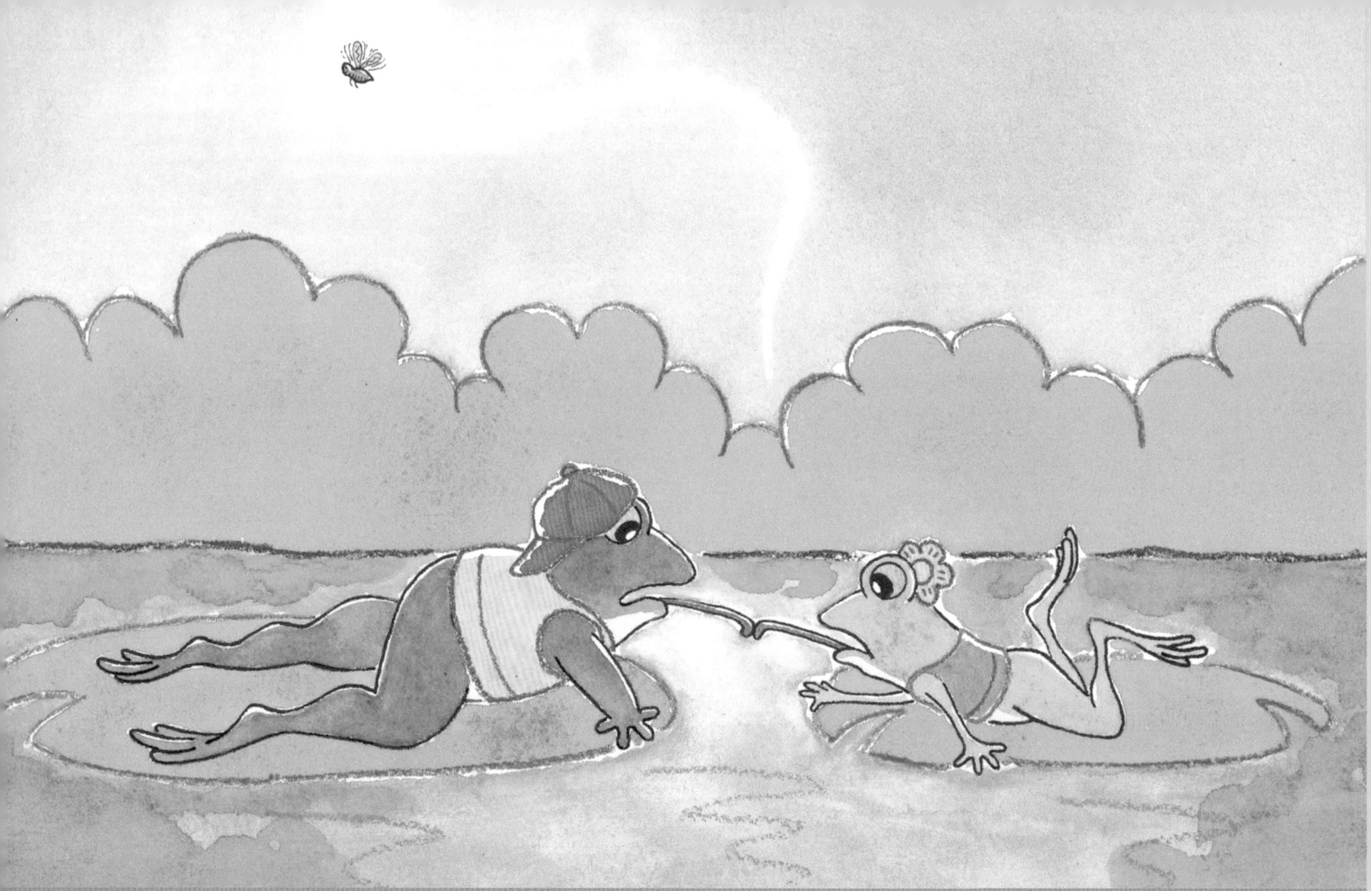

Bob and Lucy do not catch the fly.